Gooney Bird and the Room Mother

LOIS LOWRY

Illustrated by Middy Thomas

Houghton Mifflin Company Boston 2005

Walter Lorraine Books

Walter Lorraine *wr* Books

Text Copyright © 2005 by Lois Lowry
Illustrations by Middy Thomas © 2005 by Houghton Mifflin Company

www.houghtonmifflinbooks.com

Library of Congress Cataloging-in-Publication Data

Lowry, Lois.
  Gooney Bird and the room mother / by Lois Lowry ; illustrated by Middy Thomas.
      p. cm.
  "Walter Lorraine Books."
  Summary: Gooney Bird Greene, an entertaining second grader who introduces
challenging vocabulary words and tells "absolutely true" stories, finds a surprise
room mother to bring cupcakes for the Thanksgiving pageant.
  ISBN 0-618-53230-7
  [1. Thanksgiving Day—Fiction. 2. Schools—Fiction. 3. Humorous stories.] I.
Thomas, Middy Chilman, 1931- ill. II. Title.
  PZ7.L9673Gnr 2005
  [Fic]—dc22

                                                            2004015511

ISBN–13: 978-0-618-53230-8

Printed in the United States of America
WOZ 10 9 8 7 6 5 4 3 2

Gooney Bird and the Room Mother

1.

It was early November. Mrs. Pidgeon's second grade students were hard at work on their Pilgrim mural, which had been laid out on the floor. All of the desks had been pushed to one side to make room, and the second-graders were on their hands and knees, working with crayons.

Gooney Bird Greene was right in the middle, as usual.

"I like to be right smack in the middle of everything," Gooney Bird always said.

The children's shoes were lined up in the coatroom because Mrs. Pidgeon had suggested that it would be wise to take them off. If they walked on the edge of the mural, their shoes would leave marks.

"We always take our shoes off at home," Keiko had said as she untied her sneakers, "because my family came from Japan, and in Japan people never ever wear shoes in the house."

One by one the children had removed their shoes. Gooney Bird took the longest because she was wearing hiking boots that laced halfway up to her knees. When, finally, her boots were unlaced and removed, everyone could see that Gooney Bird was wearing one red sock and one yellow one.

"Gooney Bird's socks don't match!" Malcolm called out, pointing.

"Of course they don't," Gooney Bird said. "I hardly ever wear matching socks."

"Doesn't your mother roll your socks neatly into balls when she takes them out of the dryer? Doesn't she match them up very carefully?" Beanie asked.

Gooney Bird thought about that. She looked down at her own feet and wiggled her toes, one set of toes in a red sock, one in a yellow. "No," she said. "My mother puts all of my clean socks in a basket on the floor of my closet. And every day I choose two. Some days I feel like matching, but most days I don't.

"Most often," she went on, "wearing matching things gives me a feeling of ennui."

"Oh, my," said Mrs. Pidgeon. She went to the board and wrote ENNUI in big letters. "Class? You know what to do."

All of the second-graders took their dictionaries out of their desks.

At the beginning of the school year, the classroom had only one dictionary, which sat on Mrs. Pidgeon's desk, next to her coffee mug.

But Gooney Bird Greene, the new student, had arrived in October. Gooney Bird had very strong opinions about things. She had brought her own very large dictionary from home. On her first day in the classroom, she announced that she thought that every second-grader should have a very large dictionary.

Mrs. Pidgeon, who was not accustomed to Gooney Bird yet, smiled. "We've always just used this one," she said, picking up the dictionary from her desk. It was slightly dusty. "The school provided it. And it's pretty old. But the school budget doesn't allow for bigger or better dictionaries."

"If someone provided newer, more interesting dictionaries, one for each child, would you use them?" Gooney Bird asked.

Mrs. Pidgeon laughed. "Yes," she said. "Of course I would."

"Give me one week," Gooney Bird said.

Exactly one week later, a very heavy box containing twenty-two very heavy dictionaries was delivered to Mrs. Pidgeon's classroom by a man who had tattoos and big muscles. He brought the box in on a wheeled dolly.

"How on earth did you accomplish this, Gooney Bird?" Mrs. Pidgeon asked as she unpacked the dictionaries and passed one to each student.

"I planned my work," Gooney Bird said, "and then I worked my plan."

"What was your plan?" Barry Tuckerman asked as he examined his thick new dictionary.

"First I put on the right outfit."

Everyone giggled. They had known Gooney Bird Greene for only a short time, but each day she had worn a different outfit, and some of her outfits were amazing.

"What did you wear?" asked Keiko. "Pajamas and cowboy boots?" That was what Gooney Bird had worn on her first day at school.

"Of course not. This was for a businesslike visit. I wore my long, black, up-to-the-elbow gloves, my silver wet-look ski pants, a T-shirt with a picture of Albert Einstein on it, and my straw hat with a small artificial flower. I think the flower is a camellia."

"And where did you go, wearing your businesslike outfit?" Mrs. Pidgeon asked. She handed a dictionary to Tricia and reached for another.

"I went to the public library. We only just moved to the town of Watertower, as you know. But my parents have always told me that the public library is one of the first places you must visit in a new town. So I did that . . . "

"Wearing your hat with the camellia?" Mrs. Pidgeon asked.

"Yes, of course. I introduced myself to the head librarian,

the assistant librarian, the children's librarian, the reference librarian, and the janitor."

"Just the way you introduced yourself to us on the first day? I remember you said—"

All of the children remembered too. They said it together. *"My name is Gooney Bird Greene and I want a desk right smack in the middle of the room, because I like to be right smack in the middle of everything."*

"Well, why would I say that to the librarians? I didn't want a desk in the library. I wanted dictionaries."

Mrs. Pidgeon was laughing. "And so you said—"

"I said, 'I'm Gooney Bird Greene and I'm new in town and I would like to know what you do with your old dictionaries, because my second-grade class needs twenty-two of them.'"

The children all applauded. "And so they sent us the dictionaries!" Mrs. Pidgeon said in delight.

"Nope."

"Oh. Well, what happened?"

"They said that the old dictionaries were in the basement collecting dust, but they didn't have twenty-two, and also the old dictionaries were obsolete—we can look that word up after we get them all unpacked—and anyway what we needed were nice *new* dictionaries."

"These *do* look brand new," Mrs. Pidgeon said, examining one.

Gooney Bird continued. "Then, suddenly . . . "

The class grinned. They loved it when Gooney Bird said "suddenly." They waited eagerly to hear what came next.

" . . . the head librarian went to the phone and called a rich man she knew and said, 'Charles, get down here right away, because there's an enterprising young lady you must meet.'

"So a man named Charles came and shook my hand, and—"

"With your glove on? Or did you take your glove off?" Chelsea wanted to know.

"On. He shook it through my glove. Then we talked and had tea, and suddenly . . . "

Everyone grinned again, and waited.

" . . . he ordered twenty-two brand-new dictionaries, and here they are."

When the dictionaries had been distributed to every student, Mrs. Pidgeon moved the empty carton to the coatroom. "Gooney Bird Greene," she said, "you are indefatigable."

The students tried to say the word.

"Indefeat . . . "

"Undeff . . . "

"Indeteff . . . "

Mrs. Pidgeon wrote it at the top of the board, in large printing. "Class," she said, "get out your dictionaries. We will have a lesson in dictionary use."

2.

The word INDEFATIGABLE was still on the board, in the upper-right-hand corner, followed by its definition: *never showing any sign of getting tired.* Now, after the discussion about matching socks, Mrs. Pidgeon carefully wrote ENNUI at the end of the word list, because Gooney Bird had said that wearing matching socks gave her a feeling of ennui. The children knew exactly what to do when a new word appeared. They each got out a dictionary and began to look carefully through the pages.

"I found it!" Tricia called out, with her hand raised.

Mrs. Pidgeon pointed to Tricia and she read the definition aloud carefully. *"A feeling of weariness and dissatisfaction."*

"That's right," Gooney Bird said, nodding her head. "That's exactly how I feel when I wear matching socks. Weary and dissatisfied.

"May I be right smack in the middle of the Muriel, Mrs.

Pidgeon?" she asked. "I want to work on Squanto. I want to color his feather."

"It's *mural*, Gooney Bird," Mrs. Pidgeon said. "Not Muriel."

"I know that," Gooney Bird replied. "I just like to call it the Muriel. Because of Muriel Holloway in the office."

Muriel Holloway was the school secretary. She had spiked hair and fancy fingernails. If you threw up in school, first you went to the school nurse, and then Muriel Holloway called your mom to come and get you.

"May I be right smack in the middle and do Squanto?"

Mrs. Pidgeon nodded. Gooney Bird knelt in front of Squanto and began to examine her crayons.

"Everyone choose a place on the, ah, mural," Mrs. Pidgeon said. "We want to get it finished before the pageant. Nicholas, could you work on the forest in the background? Chelsea, how about you? Could you do the turkey?"

Gooney Bird had begun to color Squanto's feather blue. But all of the other children remained standing. They were all looking at their own feet. They looked weary and dissatisfied.

"My feet match," Felicia Ann whispered. "I have a feeling of ennui."

"Mine too," Tyrone said loudly. "My feet are the boringest ones in the whole room. I feel a whole lot of ennui. Can I switch one sock with Nicholas?" He sat on the floor and pulled off one white sock.

"Trade with me!" Barry Tuckerman called. He was

grabbing at Ben's left foot.

"Me!" Malcolm called loudly. "Someone switch with me!"

"My goodness, class!" Mrs. Pidgeon said. "Can we keep our voices down, please? Look how carefully Gooney Bird is coloring Squanto. We must all get busy on this mural!"

But the class wasn't listening. The children were examining their own feet and their classmates' feet. They were comparing socks and grabbing and yelling.

"You've lost them, Mrs. Pidgeon," Gooney Bird said with a sigh, "and it was my fault. I apologize. I'll try to make it up to you." She stood up. "*Class!*" she said.

Gooney Bird had a very loud voice when she wanted to use it.

"*CLASS!*" she said again.

The children looked up. They became quiet.

"Here is what we are going to do," Gooney Bird announced. "Arrange yourselves in a circle, please. Try not to step on the Muriel."

She reached out and took the hands of the children nearest to her, Tyrone on one side and Ben on the other. Tyrone reached for Chelsea. Ben took Beanie's hand. One by one the children arranged themselves in a circle around the mural.

Mrs. Pidgeon entered the circle by taking the hands of Nicholas and Chelsea and standing between them.

"Now," Gooney Bird announced, "at the count of three, we will each remove our left sock. One. Two."

"Oh, dear," Mrs. Pidgeon said, "I'm wearing pantyhose. I think I'd better drop out."

Gooney Bird nodded. "You be the supervisor," she suggested.

"Ready?" Gooney Bird said loudly. "*THREE*. Left socks off."

Every child, including Gooney Bird, removed a left sock.

"You'd better help Malcolm, Mrs. Pidgeon," Gooney Bird said. "Remember, he has that problem with left and right?"

Mrs. Pidegon nodded. She went to Malcolm and pointed out his left foot.

"Ready?" Gooney Bird said. "Everyone got that left sock off?"

The children nodded. They wiggled the toes on their bare left feet and waited for their instructions.

"At the count of three, pass your left sock to the person on your left. That will be the person beside your bare foot. Malcolm, Mrs. Pidgeon will help you. One. Two. Ready? *THREE*."

Each child handed a sock to another child.

"I got a *girl* sock," Tyrone said. "I don't want no girl sock."

"A sock is a sock," Gooney Bird said. "Anyway," she added, "you happen to have Chelsea's sock, and Chelsea is one of the smartest girls in this class. Some of her smarts may still be in that sock and they may rub off on you, Tyrone. You've got a very lucky sock there.

"Now. You can all guess what comes next, on the count of three. You put on your new sock. One. Two. *THREE*."

In a moment all the children were wearing unmatched socks. Even Gooney Bird's original pair of one red, one yellow, had become a pair of one red, one white with a blue stripe.

They all looked down and admired their feet.

"There is not a single pair of boring feet in this classroom now," Gooney Bird announced.

"Except mine," Mrs. Pidgeon said with a laugh.

"Except Mrs. Pidgeon's," Gooney Bird agreed. "Now, class, on the count of three . . . "

"Do we switch socks *again?*" Beanie asked.

"Nope. We get to work on this Muriel, because it needs to be done by the pageant. One. Two.

"THREE."

Very shortly after the count of three, when all the children had picked up their crayons and gone to work, the intercom squealed and a deep voice spoke.

"This is your principal, John Leroy. Good morning."

"Good morning," the children said to the intercom.

"We should have done this last month," Mr. Leroy explained, "or even in September. But I got busy with the selection of crossing guards, and I had to deal with certain issues and problems of playground behavior, as you know . . . "

He paused. Malcolm looked up guiltily. Malcolm had been a playground behavior problem.

" . . . but now it is definitely time to select room mothers. We will need a room mother for each classroom. Teachers, please ask your students to inquire at home. If . . . ah, just a minute . . . "

Through the intercom they could hear Muriel Holloway whispering to Mr. Leroy. Then he returned to the microphone.

"I have been reminded that last year we did have a room *father* in the third grade. Bailey Stevenson's father did an admirable job, his cupcakes were unusually fine, and we're sorry that he has found a job and is not available again this year. Well, we're not sorry that he found a job. That's not what I meant at all."

Mr. Leroy coughed and cleared his throat. "I meant that we will miss Mr. Stevenson's cupcakes. Now back to work, students. And teachers? By Friday I would like you to turn the names of the room mothers in to Muriel Holloway in the office.

"Have a good day."

The intercom squealed, buzzed, and turned silent. Carefully Gooney Bird began to color Squanto's second feather red, just beside the blue one.

Felicia Ann looked over at the one red, one blue feathers and smiled. "Like my socks," she pointed out in a whisper.

3.

"My mother says absolutely not, no way, no how," Tyrone announced. "Not unless it pays minimum wage."

Mrs. Pidgeon laughed. "Afraid not," she said. "Room mother is a volunteer job. No pay."

She looked around the room. "Did everyone ask? What did your mothers say?"

Chelsea was scowling. "My mother said if I come home wearing Nicholas's stinky dirty sock again, she's going to call Mr. Leroy and complain. And no, she won't be room mother. She already did the bake sale and she's treasurer of the PTA. Enough is enough."

"My sock was *not* stinky dirty!" Nicholas bellowed.

"No, it wasn't," Mrs. Pidgeon said. "Those were just grass stains on your sock, Nicholas. Anyone else?" She looked around. "Keiko? Maybe your mom?"

Keiko shook her head. "My mother says she is very sorry but she has to work in our store. My father needs her there."

"Yes, of course he does," Mrs. Pidgeon said. "I've been in your family's store, Keiko. Your mother works very hard.

"You all have hard-working moms, I know," she said with a smile.

"Do you have a hard-working mom, Mrs. Pidgeon?" Beanie asked.

Mrs. Pidgeon's smile turned to a sad look. "Not anymore. My mother is very, very old. She lives in a nursing home. I visit her every Sunday afternoon at the Misty Valley Elderly Care Facility. I always take her a bouquet of flowers. She seems to like that."

She looked around. "Malcolm? Did you ask your mom?"

Malcolm made a face. "My mom has trip—"

"Oh my goodness, of course she does. How could I forget that? Someone who has brand-new triplet babies at home can't possibly do anything else, and we shouldn't even have asked."

"When I asked her, she screamed," Malcolm said.

"How *are* those babies, Malcolm? How are they doing?"

"Bad," Malcolm said. "They have diarrhea."

"My goodness. No wonder she screamed. Anyone else?" asked Mrs. Pidgeon. "Beanie?"

Beanie shook her head. "My mom takes me to swimming lessons on Monday afternoon, and ballet on Tuesday, and horseback riding on Wednesday, and confirmation class on Thursday, and violin on Friday, and she says if I ask her to do one more thing . . . "

"I understand completely. Anyone else? Felicia Ann?"

Felicia Ann looked at the floor and shook her head.

"Barry?"

Barry said no.

"Nicholas?"

Nicholas was scowling. "My socks are *not* stinky dirty," he said loudly. "Chelsea's socks are stinky dirty. Chelsea's *underpants* are stinky dirty."

Chelsea hit Nicholas over the head with her spelling book.

"Enough, enough," Mrs. Pidgeon said with a sigh. She went to Nicholas and rubbed his head. She glared at Chelsea. "Let's turn to our arithmetic. We'll talk about room mothers tomorrow. All of you ask again at home. Unless . . . " She looked hopefully around the classroom one more time.

"Gooney Bird?" she asked.

Gooney Bird stood up. Today she was wearing a long velvet skirt and a sweatshirt with a picture of the earth on it.

Mrs. Pidgeon peered at the sweatshirt and smiled. "By the way, I like your shirt, Gooney Bird," she said. "Look, children, at what it says under the globe."

"Mother Earth," they all read aloud.

"We were just talking about mothers," Mrs. Pidgeon pointed out.

"Read my back," Gooney Bird said. She turned around.

They all read the back of her sweatshirt. *"Love Your Mother."*

"Well, fine," Mrs. Pidgeon said. "I wish the earth would volunteer to be room mother. Unfortunately the earth doesn't make cupcakes."

"It would make stinky dirty cupcakes," Nicholas said grouchily.

Mrs. Pidgeon glared at Nicholas. "Did you ask your mother, Gooney Bird? Not Mother Earth. Your *real* mother?" she asked.

"Yes, I tried to cajole her."

Mrs. Pidgeon started to laugh. She always laughed when Gooney Bird used a new and interesting word. She turned and wrote CAJOLE on the board. "Dictionaries, class," she said.

Beanie was the first to find *cajole* in the dictionary. "It's hard reading," she said.

"Of course it is," Mrs. Pidgeon agreed. "It's a grownup dictionary. It stretches your reading skills."

"Stretch stretch stretch," murmured Malcolm as he picked up an elastic band. Mrs. Pidgeon gave him a look. He put the elastic band down.

"Give it a try, Beanie," Mrs. Pidgeon said. "You can do it."

Beanie stood and read the definition of *cajole* slowly to the class. *"To persuade someone to do something by flattery or gentle argument, especially after a reasonable objection."*

"So your mother had a reasonable objection, Gooney Bird?" Mrs. Pidgeon asked.

"Yes. She is a terrible cook and her cupcakes are always lopsided, and also she has to go to China on Thursday."

"And so you tried to persuade her with flattery?"

"Yes, I told her that she was a wonderful cook and I had heard a rumor that she might be invited to be chef at the White House, and probably it would be good practice for her, being room mother."

"And that didn't work?" Mrs. Pidgeon was laughing.

"No, she said that if I were Pinocchio, my nose would be three feet long."

Gooney Bird scowled. "She meant I was lying, of course, but you all know that I never ever lie."

All of the children nodded. They knew that everything Gooney Bird said was absolutely true.

"I really *had* heard that rumor. I said it to myself and heard myself saying it. So it was absolutely true.

"But she said no, thank you, she did not want to be room mother, especially if she was going to work at the White House, because she wouldn't have time."

Mrs. Pidgeon pointed to the word on the board. CAJOLE.

In small handwriting she wrote its definition next to it.

"Children," she said, "tonight, please try to cajole your mothers.

"We really, really need a room mother," she said with a sigh.

❧

There was a brief knock on the classroom door, and then, without waiting for a reply to the knock, Mr. Leroy appeared. The children gasped. The principal! Usually he was only a voice on the intercom. But here he was, in person, wearing a dark blue suit and his UNICEF necktie, standing right in front of the second grade.

"Just checking in," he said cheerfully. "I was wondering if—"

Mrs. Pidgeon shook her head. "Afraid not," she said. "Not yet."

"Hmm." Mr. Leroy looked concerned. "Well," he said, "keep me posted."

He turned to leave, then stopped and said, "I like your shirt, Gooney Bird Greene."

"Thank you. Read my back." Gooney Bird turned around.

He read it and smiled. "A very fine admonition," he said. "Love your mother. Yes, indeed." Then he left the room.

"Class," said Mrs. Pidgeon, who was already writing ADMONITION on the board, "get out your dictionaries."

4.

Not a single mom wanted to be room mother. Not one.

"Oh, dear," Mrs. Pidgeon said with a sigh. She looked at the board, where the word CAJOLE was carefully printed near the end of the word list, just above ADMONITION. "I guess cajoling doesn't always work."

"Well," said Tricia from her desk, "we learned a new word, anyway. That's always a good thing."

Mrs. Pidgeon nodded. "True," she said. "And you know, class, they say that if you use a new word three times, it is yours forever."

"Who says that?" asked Beanie.

"I don't know," Mrs. Pidgeon replied. *"They."*

Barry Tuckerman stood, suddenly, beside his desk. *"Cajole, cajole, cajole,"* he said loudly. "Now it is mine forever. No one else is allowed to say it."

"That isn't exactly what I meant, Barry. You do not *own*

the word. We may all use it. And in fact, class, I wish you would all try a little more cajoling at home. This is the only class in Watertower Elementary School that does not have a room mother yet. Mr. Leroy is becoming a little impatient about it.

"Now, though, I think we ought to start our preparations for the Thanksgiving pageant. The Muriel—I mean the mural—is coming along well. But we have a song to learn, and costumes to make, and I have to select the cast."

"I already have a cast!" Ben called out, holding up his arm. Ben had fallen from his bike a month earlier and broken his wrist. All of the children, and Mrs. Pidgeon, and even the principal, Mr. Leroy, had signed their names on the cast, using different colored markers. The names were faded now, and the cast itself, which had once been white, was gray and dirty, with bits of string like dental floss dangling from it.

Keiko wrinkled her nose and said, "Your cast smells bad, Ben."

"I know," Ben said, making a face. "But next week the doctor takes it off."

"Your arm will be all skinny and wrinkled inside it when they take it off," Barry Tuckerman told him. "My cousin had a cast on his arm and his arm *died* inside the cast."

"Is that true, Mrs. Pidgeon?" Ben asked nervously.

"Your arm is probably dead already. Probably green," Barry added.

Ben's face began to pucker up. "My arm is *dead? Green?*" he wailed.

"Children, children," Mrs. Pidgeon said. "No, Ben, your arm will be fine. Besides, I'm talking about a different kind of cast. We need a cast of characters for the pageant. We need Pilgrims and Native Americans. We also need a turkey, and, let me see, some succotash, and a pumpkin pie. But the food items don't have to be human beings."

"I want to be Squanto!" Gooney Bird said. "I love Squanto. He was always absolutely right smack in the middle of everything."

"Squanto's a *boy!*" Barry called loudly. "Only a boy can be Squanto! Right, Mrs. Pidgeon?"

"Actually," Mrs. Pidgeon said, "I've already made a list. So put your hands down, everyone."

She read the list aloud. There were twenty-two children in the classroom, and each was on the list. Eleven Pilgrims. Eleven Native Americans.

"But who is Squanto?" the children asked.

Mrs. Pidgeon looked around the class. Now every child, not just Gooney Bird and Barry, was waving an arm in the air, volunteering eagerly to be Squanto.

"I haven't decided that yet," Mrs. Pidgeon said. "But I have an idea."

She went to the board, to the list of words.

REWARD, she wrote. "You all know what a reward is," Mrs. Pidgeon said.

"Money!" shouted Ben. "A thousand dollars if you catch a criminal!"

"Well," Mrs. Pidgeon said, "it could be that. But a reward doesn't have to be about criminals. Let's look it up."

Everyone opened the dictionaries and turned the pages. Chelsea raised her hand first. *"That which is given in appreciation,"* she read aloud to the class.

"You see, it doesn't have to be money," Mrs. Pidgeon explained. "And in this case, the reward I am going to give is the important role of Squanto in the pageant. Someone is going to get that role in appreciation. It will be that person's reward."

"Reward for what?" several children asked at the same time. "For catching a criminal?"

"No," Mrs Pidgeon said. She sighed. "For finding me a room mother."

❧

An hour later, after lunch, the second-graders were learning one of the songs for the Thanksgiving pageant. It was a complicated song that Mrs. Pidgeon herself had written. The Pilgrims sang half and the Native Americans sang half. The song was about food.

"Succotash, succotash, lima beans and corn . . ." Mrs.

Pidgeon played the notes on the piano and sang the words. "To the tune of 'Jingle Bells,'" she explained. "Ready, Native Americans? This is your part. Try it with me."

Eleven children, including Gooney Bird Greene, sang the succotash lines.

"Now, Pilgrims? Listen to your part. Just like the next two lines of 'Jingle Bells.'" Mrs. Pidgeon played and sang, *"Thank you for the vegetables, On this Thanksgiving morn."*

The Pilgrims sang loudly.

"Now the next verse is about the turkey. Native Americans? Ready to listen carefully?"

Gooney Bird Greene raised her hand. "Does Squanto sing with the Native Americans?" she asked.

"No, actually, while the Pilgrims and Native Americans are singing, Squanto will be carrying the food across the stage. Perhaps Squanto will do some sort of dance. I haven't worked out the details yet."

Beanie, standing with the Pilgrims, raised her hand. "I take ballet lessons!" she said. "Maybe I could be—"

But Mrs. Pidgeon shook her head. "Not ballet, Beanie," she said. "They didn't have ballet in Plymouth. All right, class, let's pay careful attention to the next part. Still the tune of 'Jingle Bells,' remember. *Gobble gobble, here it comes, turkey roasted brown . . .*" She played the melody on the piano while she sang the words. Then the eleven Native Americans sang it after her.

"Mrs. Pidgeon, may I please be excused?" Gooney Bird asked politely. "I need to be excused."

Mrs. Pidgeon paused with her hands on the piano keys. "Is this a seriously urgent need?" she asked.

"Yes."

"All right, then. Be quick."

Gooney Bird slipped out of the classroom while Mrs. Pidgeon sang on. *"Thank you, noble Squanto, you may set the platter dooooowwnn . . . "*

The children were still singing and passing imaginary helpings of food around when Gooney Bird returned a few minutes later.

"Announcement!" Gooney Bird said in a loud voice. "Important announcement!"

Mrs. Pidgeon stopped playing the piano. The room became quiet. All of the children knew that when Gooney Bird had an announcement to make, it was worth listening to.

"I am Squanto," Gooney Bird announced.

"But—" Mrs. Pidgeon began.

"I got us a room mother," Gooney Bird said proudly.

Mrs. Pidgeon clapped her hands. "But how?" she asked.

"Simple phone call. They let me use the telephone in the office. I told Muriel Holloway it was an emergency."

Mrs. Pidgeon frowned slightly. "Well," she said, "it was beginning to feel like an emergency, actually."

"So now I'm Squanto, right?"

"Wait, Gooney Bird! You haven't told us *who* our room mother is!"

"I'll write it down," Gooney Bird Greene said. She went to the board and picked up the chalk. "Class," she said, "get out your dictionaries." She wrote a word very carefully on the board, at the end of the list.

The word she wrote was INCOGNITO.

"This is our room mother's name," she said.

5.

"*With the identity disguised or hidden,*" Mrs. Pidgeon read to the class, from the dictionary. "So our room mother doesn't want us to know who she is?

"Or *he?*" she added, remembering Bailey Stevenson's father.

"It's a she," Gooney Bird said. "I think it's okay to tell you that. But you're right: she wants to be a secret."

"How did you cajole her?" Tricia asked. "Is it *my* mom? I couldn't cajole her. How did you?"

"Is it *mine?*" Barry asked. "I bet it's mine."

"Did you pay her?" Tyrone asked. "If you paid her, it's *mine.*"

"My lips are sealed," Gooney Bird said.

"Maybe it's mine," Keiko said.

"Maybe *mine,*" whispered Felicia Ann. "Oh, I hope mine."

Malcolm was rolling a piece of paper into a tube that looked like a telescope. Malcolm had a very hard time keeping his hands still. He called out loudly, "If it's my mom, and if she brings those three babies to this school, I'm . . . I'm . . . " He scowled and sputtered and wrinkled his face and couldn't decide just what he would do.

"Sealed," Gooney Bird repeated.

"What are your babies' names?" Felicia Ann asked Malcolm. "I love babies."

"I'm not saying," Malcolm replied with a scowl. "My lips are sealed."

Mrs. Pidgeon began to laugh. "Well, class, Malcolm is not going to reveal the triplets' names. And Gooney Bird is not going to reveal the identity of our room mother, though I somehow suspect that it might be someone who has decided that she doesn't want to be chef at the White House . . ."

She looked at Gooney Bird, who shook her head. "Tightly sealed," she said.

"Well, I am delighted that we have one," Mrs. Pidgeon said, "and I will notify Mr. Leroy. But Gooney Bird, would you tell us—without revealing the name, of course—the absolutely true story of how you cajoled her?"

Gooney Bird nodded. "I guess I could do that," she said. She was already standing in the center of the room, and she began to take deep breaths, as she always did when beginning a story.

The Pilgrims and Native Americans all sat down on the

floor. Keiko clapped her hands in delight. Malcolm stopped rolling the piece of paper into a tube. Barry crept over to his desk and sat down quietly. Mrs. Pidgeon turned around on the piano bench to listen.

"'How Gooney Bird Got a Room Mother' is the title," Gooney Bird began.

"Sometimes," she explained, "a title should be a little mysterious. It should make you wonder what the story is about. I could have called this one 'An Exciting Phone Call' or maybe . . ."

"'Incognito'!" called Barry from his desk. "That would have been a good title!"

Gooney Bird nodded. "Yes, it would. Good for you, Barry. I might change my title later, actually. You can do that. The title you use first is called the *working* title. And my working title is 'How Gooney Bird Got a Room Mother.' "

She looked down at herself. "You know how usually, in stories, I try to describe what the main character looks like, and what she is wearing?"

The children nodded. They had heard Gooney Bird tell many stories before.

"Well," she said, "in this story, the main character is me, and as you can see, today I am wearing tap shoes, blue tights, red Bermuda shorts, and an embroidered peasant blouse from Bavaria."

"Bavaria!" murmured Felicia Ann. "I never heard of Bavaria before!"

"It's quite an interesting outfit, I think," Gooney Bird said. "But I've decided that it will not be included in the story. This story is going to be an all-dialogue story. No description."

"Class?" Mrs. Pidgeon said. She went to the board and wrote the word DIALOGUE. For a few moments the room was silent except for the pages of the dictionaries turning.

"I found it!" called Ben. He read aloud, *"Words used by characters in a book."*

"Or a story," Gooney Bird said. "Okay. I'm going to begin. There are only two characters in this story. One is Gooney Bird, and the other is . . ."

"Oh, don't tell! She doesn't want you to tell!" several children called.

". . . Mrs. X," Gooney Bird said. "I'm calling her Mrs. X. And I'm starting my story with a sound effect. Listen."

RINNNNG. RINNNNG.

"Hello?" Mrs. X said, when she answered the telephone.

"Hello," said Gooney Bird Greene. "I am calling from Watertower Elementary School."

"Yes? My goodness, is something wrong at the school?" asked Mrs. X.

"I think it was my mom," Keiko said. "She always worries. She worries about chicken pox, and unsanitary restrooms, and earthquakes."

"My mom worries too," said Tricia. "Mine worries about kidnappers and unfriendly dogs."

"Mine worries about undercooked hamburger," said Ben.

"Mine too. And swimming too soon after lunch. And wasps," said Chelsea.

"Not mine," Malcolm said glumly. "My mom only worries about those triplets. And diaper rash."

"Please tell their names, Malcolm. I love babies," Felicia Ann said in her soft voice.

"No. They're incognito."

"Class!" Gooney Bird said impatiently. "You are interrupting the story! Dialogue is supposed to flow along smoothly!"

"Sorry," everyone replied.

"But you did remind me of something: how much all moms worry about their children. So I'm going to interrupt the dialogue and insert something about that."

"What's that called, when you do that?" asked Beanie.

Gooney Bird thought, and then shrugged. "I don't know," she said. She looked at the teacher. "Mrs. Pidgeon?"

Mrs. Pidgeon thought. Then she said, "That would be called an *authorial intrusion,* I think. When the author intrudes to say something that really isn't part of the story. But I'm not even going to write that on the board. It isn't important."

"Well, here I go, starting up again!" Gooney Bird said. She took a deep breath and continued.

All mothers worry about their children. Not only human mothers, but animals. Once I had a cat who was always looking for her kittens and got very upset if they strayed too far away. Now picture if that cat was a *human* and her children went to school every day and she didn't know what was going on at school, and suddenly someone called and said . . .

Gooney Bird stopped and looked around. Malcolm had started rolling his paper again, and Felicia Ann, seated on the floor, had put her head down on her knees. Chelsea yawned.

"Sorry," Gooney Bird said. "That is why authors shouldn't intrude. It's boring. Back to the dialogue."

"No, Mrs. X," said Gooney Bird. "There is nothing to worry about. I am calling with a request."

"And what might that be? Not a solicitation for money, I hope!" Mrs. X's voice sounded suspicious.

"I bet it's my mom!" said Beanie. "She hates when the phone rings and it's someone—"
Gooney Bird glared at Beanie.
"Sorry," Beanie said.

"No, I'm calling to tell you that you have been selected for a great honor."
"*Right!* The last time I got a call like that, they told me I had won a trip to Las Vegas," Mrs. X said, "but then it turned out that I was supposed to pay taxes and handling charges and buy a membership in something, I think a health club . . ."

"It's my mother," Barry announced loudly. "I'm sure it's my mother."
"No, it's mine," said Tyrone. "She almost bought a time-share in Mexico and it was a big scam."
"It's *my* mother," Nicholas and Tricia said together.
Gooney Bird glared at all of them. When the room fell silent, she continued.

Gooney Bird explained very patiently. "No," she

said, "this is truly a great honor, not a scam at all. You have been chosen as room mother for Mrs. Pidgeon's second-grade class."

Mrs. X was silent for a moment. She was dumbfounded. She was overcome.

"Are you still there?" Gooney Bird asked.

"Yes," said Mrs. X.

"So may I tell everyone you said that?"

"Said what?" asked Mrs. X.

" 'Yes.' You said, 'Yes.' "

"I only meant, 'Yes, I am still here.' "

"Please, please say yes," Gooney Bird said, "because then I get to be Squanto."

Mrs. X still didn't speak.

"And the principal will stop bugging Mrs. Pidgeon," Gooney Bird added.

"The principal is doing that?" asked Mrs. X in an outraged voice.

"Indeed he is," Gooney Bird replied.

Mrs. X didn't speak.

"The only thing you have to do is provide cupcakes. And you can come to the Thanksgiving pageant if you want, and sit in a seat of honor, and also—"

Gooney Bird looked at Mrs. Pidgeon. "I hope you don't mind, I said the next thing without asking your permission."

"What was that?" Mrs. Pidgeon asked. "I hope you didn't say she'd be paid. You know we don't pay anything."

"I'll continue," Gooney Bird said.

"And also, Mrs. Pidgeon, who wrote quite a fine song about succotash, will compose a second song, and its title will be 'Room Mother.'"

Mrs. Pidgeon began to laugh. "All right," she said. "I can do that."

Gooney Bird looked relieved. She continued.

"And," Gooney Bird told Mrs. X, "we will all sing the song to you at the end of the Thanksgiving pageant."

There was silence on the other end of the telephone. Then—

Gooney Bird looked at the class. "Guess the next word," she said.

"SUDDENLY!" they all shouted out. They'd learned from Gooney Bird how important the word *suddenly* could be.

"You got it." Gooney Bird continued.

Suddenly Mrs. X started to laugh. And she said, "Yes. I'll do it."

"Thank you, thank you!" Gooney Bird told her.

"On one condition," Mrs. X added.

"What is that?"

"Until Thanksgiving, I am incognito."

"My lips are sealed," said Gooney Bird.

The End

The class clapped. Gooney Bird bowed. Mrs. Pidgeon smiled.

"Gooney Bird," she said, "you are Squanto, for sure."

6.

"Why do we have to have cardboard costumes?" Beanie complained. "At ballet class, we have stretchy satin, and for the recital I have shimmery wings attached. They're gold."

"Hold still," Mrs. Pidgeon told her. "I have to cut this very carefully. I don't want to miss and cut your hair."

Beanie stood very, very still. She looked nervous. "Don't you dare," she said. "I'm growing my hair to my waist."

"Ha!" shouted Malcolm. "Beanie's hair goes to the waste! To the *wastebasket!*"

"There," Mrs. Pidgeon said. "You can move now, Bean." She lifted the white cardboard that she had been cutting. "The reason we have cardboard costumes is because we already have cardboard, so it doesn't cost anything. And it makes good Pilgrim hats and Native American headbands.

"Malcolm." She glared at him. "Stop tormenting Beanie. Is your belt buckle almost finished?"

Malcolm nodded and went back to his work. All of the Pilgrim boys were making large cardboard belt buckles. "I saw a guy with a skull on his belt buckle," he announced. "He was a Hell's Angel."

"Cool!" said Ben. "A real skull?"

"No. Fake."

Keiko looked up from the beads she was gluing onto her Native American headband. "Don't talk about skulls," she said nervously. "It makes me feel sick."

"My mom has skull earrings," Tyrone announced. "She wore them on Halloween. They dangled. Two little skulls."

Keiko stopped gluing beads and put her hands over her ears.

"These belt buckles will be very plain," Mrs. Pidgeon said. "The Pilgrims didn't decorate their clothing. The Native Americans did, though. Look what a good job Keiko is doing." Gently she reached down and removed Keiko's hands from her ears so that Keiko could continue attaching beads before her glue dried.

"Me too! Look at mine!" Tricia held up her headband.

"And mine! Mine's the best!" Nicholas called.

Mrs. Pidgeon walked around the room admiring the work of each second-grader. "I'm proud of all of you," she said, smiling. "Pilgrim girls, even though you don't have decorations, your white bonnets are quite lovely. Chelsea," she said, adjusting Chelsea's cardboard hat, "I think you might want to trim yours back a bit so that it doesn't cover your eyes that way.

"And Native Americans? When you finish your beading, you may each add one feather from the feather pile." She reached for Tyrone's hand, which had quickly grabbed the entire collection of feathers. "Just one, Tyrone. Remember we talked about sharing just yesterday?"

Scowling, Tyrone selected a long yellow feather and put the rest back.

"I wish I could be a Native American," Chelsea said, frowning. "I hate my Pilgrim hat. It's too plain."

Beanie, wearing her white cardboard bonnet, patted Chelsea's arm. "But we were very brave," she reminded her. "We crossed the ocean, remember? And not in a cruise ship, either."

Ben, looking up from under the brim of his tall black Pilgrim hat, added, "Feathers are for babies. Pilgrims were tough and mean. They battled pirates."

"Actually," Mrs. Pidgeon said, "I don't think the Pilgrims encountered pirates at sea. But they certainly were brave. You're right about that, Ben. Can you lift your hat up a little, so your eyes show?"

Ben tilted his head back so that he could see. All of the Pilgrims had their heads tilted back. Somehow the Pilgrim hats were all a little too large.

"Good work, everyone!" Mrs. Pidgeon continued, looking around at the class. "And you've all memorized the words to the food song?"

All of the Native Americans and Pilgrims nodded.

"We'll practice it again when we get the headgear all done."

"Have you written the room mother song, Mrs. Pidgeon?" Gooney Bird asked. She was coloring Squanto's headband carefully.

"I'm working on it. There's a little problem with rhyming," Mrs. Pidgeon said. "If only she'd let us use her *name*—"

"Absolutely not," Gooney Bird said. "Incognito."

"Well, if you'd explain to her what a problem it creates. For example," Mrs. Pidgeon said, "if the song went, *Hail to thee, Room Mother Greene,* then the next line could easily be *Best room mother we've ever seen*—"

Gooney Bird Greene stopped coloring. She glared at Mrs. Pidgeon.

"I just used that as an example," Mrs. Pidgeon explained hastily. "I didn't intend to give anything away. I could have used a different example. *Room Mother Brown*, for instance. *Best room mother in town*—"

Gooney Bird put her hands on her hips. "I talked to her last night, and she said that if anyone says her name, if anyone reveals her identity, she will *not* bring cupcakes and she will not even come to the pageant, no matter how many songs you write."

"Well then, she will remain incognito." Mrs. Pidgeon laughed. "And I'll create the best song I can, under the circumstances."

"Thank you."

"And what about Squanto's dance, Gooney Bird? Have you been working on it?"

Gooney Bird frowned. "Yes. It's hard, though. I keep wanting to do the hula."

"The *hula?*"

"My grandma can do the hula," Keiko said. "She lives in Hawaii."

"That's lovely, Keiko. If she comes to visit, maybe she can give us lessons," Mrs. Pidgeon said.

"*My* grandma can do the funky chicken!" Chelsea said. She stood, with her white Pilgrim hat falling forward, in order to demonstrate.

"Gross!" Nicholas and Ben said together, watching Chelsea wiggle her behind.

Mrs. Pidgeon played a loud chord on the piano in order to get the class's attention. Then she began to play some low notes in a repetitive way. "Pretend this is a drumbeat, Gooney Bird. Squanto should simply move across the stage, keeping time to the sound of drums. Maybe some rhythmic foot-hopping too?"

"I guess so," Gooney Bird said. "I'll work on it at home. And it'll be easier when I have my costume on. I'll feel more like a real Squanto in my costume. I'll feel authentic, then."

Mrs. Pidgeon picked up the chalk and added AUTHENTIC to the word list.

"True and original, known to be trustworthy," Beanie read from her dictionary.

"That's Squanto, all right," said Gooney Bird.

7.

"I've got the room mother song finished," Mrs. Pidgeon announced. She sat down at the piano. "We'll need to learn it quickly because, as you know, the Thanksgiving pageant is next week.

"Gather round," she said. "And now that we've finished the hats and headbands, why don't we wear them while we sing? This will be a sort of a dress rehearsal.

"Pilgrims over here." She pointed to the left. "And Native Americans here." She pointed to the right. The second-graders, wearing their headgear, arranged themselves around the piano.

"I can't see!" Nicholas called. His Pilgrim hat had slid down over his eyes. Beanie, her own white bonnet falling across her forehead, leaned over and lifted his hat up. "Stand very still," she told him, "so it doesn't fall down again."

"How about me?" Gooney Bird asked. "Where should Squanto stand? Probably in the middle, right? Because he's the star, right smack in the middle of everything?"

"In the middle is fine," Mrs. Pidgeon said. "What is that on your head, Gooney Bird?"

"Squanto's hat."

"I thought you were making a headband. I *saw* you making a headband."

"I decided Squanto should have a better hat than the other Native Americans, because he's been to England, remember?"

"Well, yes, he did travel there. But that's a top hat, Gooney Bird. Something an ambassador might wear. I don't think—"

"I think Squanto brought it back from England. He probably went shopping and bought a lot of new clothes there. People always buy new clothes when they travel."

"That's true. My mom went to Hawaii to visit my grandma, and she bought a muumuu," Keiko said.

"My dad went to Albuquerque on business and he brought back a silver and turquoise belt buckle," Tricia said.

"My mom and dad went . . ." Chelsea began.

Mrs. Pidgeon sighed. She played a chord on the piano, to quiet the children. Then she played a simple melody.

She played it again, and sang, *"Roooommmm Motherrrr—"*

She looked around. "Recognize that? It's the melody from 'Moon River.' "

All of the second-graders shook their heads. "I know a song about the man in the moon," Beanie said.

"I know one about the cow that jumped over the moon," Ben said.

"I know one about shine on harvest moon," Nicholas said.

"I know a moon song," Tyrone announced. "Listen! *Oh Mister Moon, Moon, bright and shiny moon, please shine down on meeeee!*"

"No, no." Mrs. Pidgeon played the melody again. "*Roooommmm Motherrrr,*" she sang. "Try it with me."

"*Roooommmm Motherrrr,*" all of the children sang. Keiko's headband fell forward across her eyes. She pushed it back up but her bangs got caught.

"I can't see," Felicia Ann whispered. Her Pilgrim bonnet had lurched down over her forehead.

"Oh dear," Mrs. Pidgeon said, turning around on the piano bench. "We're having hat problems of all sorts. Let's not worry about that now, though. We need to learn this song. The next line is . . . " She hesitated. "Well, if we were singing the original song, it would be *wider than a mile*—but of course we don't want the room mother to think we are commenting on how *wide* she is, do we?" Mrs. Pidgeon winked at Gooney Bird.

Gooney Bird shrugged. "I don't think she'd mind," she said.

"I've changed it," Mrs. Pidgeon said. "So we'll sing *kinder than a smile* instead. Give it a try after me, class."

The Pilgrims and Native Americans all sang loudly. *"Kinder than a smile—"*

"Good! Barry? Can you push your headband up?"

Barry tried.

"Ben? Pilgrim hat? Up?"

Ben tried. He wrinkled his face in order to hold his hat brim up.

"Next line: *Your clothing is in style—*"

"Why would we say that, Mrs. Pidgeon?" Gooney Bird asked.

"Well, because it rhymes with *smile*. And although of course I don't *know* our room mother, although she's incognito, I suspect she is quite stylish, right? Because she comes from a stylish family?"

Mrs. Pidgeon looked meaningfully at Gooney Bird, who today was wearing a long flowered gypsy skirt, a leather vest, hiking boots with red laces, and, of course, the top hat that she had explained Squanto would have brought back from his stay in England.

Gooney Bird sighed. "Okay," she said. "Whatever."

"Hooray—" Mrs. Pidgeon sang next. "In the original song,"

she explained, "it says *someday* at that point. But *someday* doesn't work for us, really."

"No," said Malcolm loudly, "because we'll want those cupcakes *right away* after the pageant!"

"Let's try that first verse again from the beginning. Nicholas? Can you see, with your Pilgrim hat down like that?"

"No," said Nicholas from under his hat brim. "But it's okay. I can sing."

"Roooommmm Motherrrr," the second-graders sang enthusiastically, in unison.

Wearing her top hat jauntily and singing as loudly as possible, Gooney Bird began testing some dance steps in the center of the room. "I think Squanto probably learned the tango in England," she explained.

8.

On Tuesday morning of Thanksgiving week, the day before the pageant, Mrs. Pidgeon wrote another new word on the board, below AUTHENTIC. She wrote FIASCO. She sighed, and stared at the word.

"Dictionaries, class," she instructed, though she hadn't needed to. The second-graders had already reached for their dictionaries and begun turning to the *F* section.

Barry Tuckerman waved his hand in the air. "I found it!" he called out. When Mrs. Pidgeon nodded to Barry, he stood and read aloud, *"A total failure."*

Mrs. Pidgeon sighed. "Correct, Barry. Good dictionary work. The word *fiasco* means a total failure, especially a humiliating one. Say it after me, class."

"Fiasco. Fiasco. Fiasco," the second-graders said aloud.

The gerbils, usually quiet in their cage in the corner, unexpectedly began to fight. They chittered noisily and chased each other in a circle. A paper thumbtacked to the bulletin board suddenly came loose and fluttered to the floor. The radiator hissed. Outside, it was raining in a steady drizzle.

"What's wrong, Mrs. Pidgeon?" asked Beanie. "You look sad. Did we do something wrong?"

"No, no. You children have all worked so hard. I'm very proud of you," Mrs. Pidgeon said. "But I'm worried about the Thanksgiving pageant," she confessed. "I'm afraid it will be a fiasco."

"No, it won't! Look! I got my cast off!" Ben reminded her, holding up his arm. "And my arm works!"

"We sent the invitations," said Felicia Ann. "And, remember, we put turkey stamps on them?"

"The Muriel's done," Barry pointed out. "It turned out great! We only have to hang it up in the multipurpose room."

"The room mother says the cupcakes are all ready for tomorrow afternoon," Gooney Bird said. "And lemonade."

"Yes, you've all done wonderfully. And all of your mothers are coming? I know yours is, of course, Gooney Bird," Mrs. Pidgeon said. "Everyone else? And some dads? And little brothers and sisters?"

All of the children nodded. "And my auntie," Keiko said.

"And my triplets," Malcolm said, making a face. "I hoped they would get chicken pox, but they didn't."

"Please, *please* tell me their names," Felicia Ann begged.

"No," Malcolm said with a scowl. "They don't *have* names."

"Malcolm, Malcolm," Mrs. Pidgeon said, putting her arm gently across his shoulders. "They probably have beautiful names and I hope someday you will tell them to us.

"You children have all worked very hard. It's just that—" She hesitated.

"What?" asked Beanie. "We know all the words to the songs."

"Well, I'm concerned about the songs," Mrs. Pidgeon said. "I'm not really a songwriter, and they seem, well, a little slapdash to me."

She wrote the word on the board.

"Oh, dear," said Ben when he found it in the dictionary. "That's bad."

"I know," Mrs. Pidgeon said, and she wrote the definition on the board: *"Careless, hasty, unskillful."*

"Our costumes are all made," Tricia added.

"I'm very concerned about the costumes," Mrs. Pidgeon said. "I'm not really a costume designer, and they seem—"

"Slapdash?" asked Tyrone.

"Maybe a little," Mrs. Pidgeon said, "and ill-fitting."

"We know our lines," Nicholas said. "Mine is 'Thank you, good friend Squanto!' I know it by heart."

"I'm concerned about the lines," Mrs. Pidgeon said.

"But you wrote the lines, Mrs. Pidgeon!" Tricia pointed out.

"I know. And I'm not really a writer. The lines are slap-dash."

All of the children looked at Mrs. Pidgeon. She looked very sad. Felicia Ann, the most bashful person in the class, went to her and gave her a hug. "You're a very good teacher, Mrs. Pidgeon," she said. "You don't have to be a writer, or a songwriter, or a costume designer, or even a Muriel maker. Because you're a *teacher*. You taught me to *read!*"

"Me too!" called Tyrone. "I couldn't read worth *nuthin'* when I came to this class! Now lookit! I can read a whole dictionary!"

"Me too!" called Ben. "I only could read baby books before, but now I can read whole long words!"

"We all can!" the other children shouted.

Mrs. Pidgeon began to cheer up. She smiled at the children. "Thank you," she said. "I'm sorry that I was depressed for a minute. It's just that the story of the first Thanksgiving is such a truly wonderful story, about becoming friends, and helping one another, and being thankful. I wish I could have presented it better, instead of writing a dumb song about succotash."

"Mrs. Pidgeon?" Gooney Bird Greene said. "I have an idea."

9.

It was the day before Thanksgiving vacation—the day of the pageant. The school janitor, Lester Furillo, had used masking tape to attach the mural to the wall of the multipurpose room, and he had set up folding chairs for the audience. At the back of the large room, a table covered with a yellow paper tablecloth held two large platters of cupcakes and two pitchers of lemonade.

"These cupcakes are spectacular!" Mrs. Pidgeon had said when she opened the boxes that held them. "Look at this! Little turkeys and Pilgrim hats on the frosting! How did she ever do that, Gooney Bird?"

"She didn't do it," Gooney Bird replied. "You saw who brought them. You saw the name on the van. I think it's on the boxes too."

"Creative Catering," Beanie read from the lid of one box.

"I thought the room mother was supposed to make the cupcakes herself," Tricia said.

Gooney Bird shook her head. "I just told her to *provide* cupcakes. Remember the dialogue from when I told the story about getting the room mother? She asked what the room mother had to do, and I said provide cupcakes. You all know what *provide* means. We don't even need to get out our dictionaries."

"Well," Mrs. Pidgeon said as she arranged the cupcakes on a platter, "she certainly did a good job of providing, didn't she? But I wish she had brought them herself. I'd like to thank her."

"She's coming to the pageant," Gooney Bird assured her.

❧

And now, in the afternoon, the guests were arriving. The second-graders were all in the small adjoining room, peeking out, watching the chairs in the multipurpose room fill up.

"There's my mom!" Tyrone said in an excited voice. "Lookit! She's got such a cool dress on!

"Mom!" he called. "I'm back here!" Tyrone's mother looked over with a grin and waved.

"Shhh!" the other children said. "Nobody's supposed to see us yet!"

"This is the dressing room!" Ben explained. "We're backstage! We have to be quiet. Hey!" he added. "Look! There's *my* mom!"

"My daddy came!" Keiko said, peeking out. "He must have closed the store for the afternoon! Look—there he is with my mom. And see? That's my auntie! Hello, Oba-chan!" she called, and a woman laughed and fluttered her fingers in a wave.

Mrs. Pidgeon had been at the door of the multipurpose room, greeting the guests. Now she came back to where the children were waiting. "I hear some giggling back here!" she said with a smile.

"Are you all ready?" she asked. "We'll start in a few minutes. Not quite everyone is here yet. The room mother hasn't arrived."

"She said she might be a little late," Gooney Bird explained. "She said we could start without her. Oh, look!" Gooney Bird pointed. "There's my mom! See? She's the one in jeans, with a smiley face sweatshirt."

She wiggled her fingers in a wave, and her mother waved back and took a seat.

There was a sudden commotion at the door of the multipurpose room, and several people got up from their seats to help. Malcolm looked, and groaned. "It's my mom," he said, "with the triplets." He covered his eyes. "I'm not going to look," he said.

Mrs. Pidgeon put her arm around Malcolm. She and the

other children watched while the janitor and several others helped to maneuver the huge triple stroller through the doorway.

"Are they asleep?" Malcolm asked, still hiding his eyes. "Please, please, could they be asleep?"

"Yes, they seem to be sleeping, Malcolm. It's okay. You can look. Don't worry," Mrs. Pidgeon told him. "We won't even mind if they wake up. We *like* babies."

"I love babies," whispered Felicia Ann. "I hope those triplets wake up so I can hold them."

"They always smell bad," Malcolm whispered back. He stuck out his tongue and crossed his eyes.

꙯

Mrs. Pidgeon went to the piano at the front of the multi-purpose room and played a few chords to make people stop talking. It was what she did in the classroom, and it always worked there. It worked here too, with the grownups. They all became silent.

Mr. Leroy walked to the front of the room. The multipurpose room didn't have a stage. But he stood in front of the audience, wearing a necktie today with a plump turkey on it, and he spoke in a loud, clear voice, just the way Mrs. Pidgeon had told the children that they should.

The second-graders listened from behind the cracked-open door to their dressing room.

"Good afternoon, ladies and gentlemen," Mr. Leroy said. "I'm delighted to see so many parents here today, and some grandparents, I see, and even a few little brothers and sisters."

"And an auntie," whispered Keiko.

"Are your triplets brothers or sisters?" Felicia Ann asked Malcolm.

"Shhh," Malcolm said. "I'm not saying."

"And perhaps our new room mother as well?" Mr. Leroy said in a cheerful voice, looking around the audience. "Would the second-grade room mother like to stand?

"Maybe she's a little shy," he went on when no one stood. "But she certainly did provide wonderful refreshments, which we will enjoy after the performance.

"Speaking of the performance, I would like to mention that this is the fifth and final Thanksgiving pageant today. I watched the kindergarten children this morning—they did quite a lively dance during which they gobbled like turkeys and flapped imaginary wings. It was a little noisier than we had expected, but we got it under control after a bit, and I think we learned quite a bit about how dangerous wing-flapping can be, actually. For those of you who heard about it and are worried, incidentally, little Chloe McAllister is going to be fine. Nothing more than a fat lip."

Mr. Leroy straightened his tie. "After that," he went on, "the fourth grade performed quite an impressive play about

Captain Miles Standish, who arrived on the *Mayflower*, and the great Indian Massasoit who became his friend.

"Unfortunately, Jason Carruthers and Jeffrey Hall, who were to play the roles of Miles Standish and Massasoit, are both absent today because there seems to be a stomach virus making the rounds. The other fourth graders, though, did a great job of explaining what the play would have been like if the leading characters had been available.

"Next, the first grade had worked very hard on learning all the words of the traditional Thanksgiving song 'We Gather Together,' and they sang it with remarkable enthusiasm for the audience. Unfortunately their teacher had not taken into account how difficult the lines *'He chastens and hastens his will to make known, The wicked oppressing now cease from distressing . . .'* would be for people whose front teeth had recently fallen out, and I believe that was fourteen of the eighteen first-graders. But their gusto made up for their pronunciation.

"Then, finally, just an hour ago, we had the third grade's very colorful reenactment of the first Thanksgiving dinner. The third grade is so fortunate that one father provided large cardboard cartons, one for each performer to wear, with their heads of course emerging from the tops of the cartons, and each decorated as a type of food—squash, corn, potatoes, and the like. The third graders got most of the way through a recitation and demonstration of the various courses of that dinner. I think, actually, that it might have been the food descriptions that brought on an onslaught of the stomach virus mid-performance, so that we had some unfortunate events, during which we had to extricate several children quickly from their cartons, and we ended up with a very slippery floor—"

"Both of the DeMarco twins threw up," Barry Tuckerman announced to the other children. "Identical throw-ups. I heard the janitor telling Muriel Holloway."

"Oh, no!" wailed Keiko.

"Shhh," Gooney Bird said.

"—but our hardworking custodian, Lester Furillo, has taken care of that," Mr. Leroy went on, "and with the help of some air-freshener I think we're in good shape for our final performance of the day, from Mrs. Pidegon's second grade.

"Thank you again for coming. I see someone else is just arriving. Is that another stroller?" He peered toward the back. "My goodness! So many vehicles today! Lester Furillo will help you in. There are still some seats in the back. Please make yourself comfortable." Mr. Leroy gestured toward the chairs in the back as more people entered. Then he turned to the piano and said, "Mrs. Pidgeon? It's all yours!"

Mrs. Pidgeon smiled. She played a verse of "We Gather Together" to call the crowd to attention and create a Thanksgiving mood. Then she nodded to Gooney Bird, who was in the doorway waiting for her cue to enter.

10.

While Mrs. Pidgeon played a rhythmic, drumming sort of music on the piano, Gooney Bird Greene danced from the door to the front of the multipurpose room. Her dance was a combination of shuffles, taps, and twirls, with an occasional pause for a hop. She was wearing fuzzy bedroom slippers, her long velvet skirt, a flowered Hawaiian shirt, and a top hat, onto which she had attached a blue feather.

The audience applauded at her entrance.

She ended her dance and bowed dramatically, steadying her hat with one hand.

"I am Squanto," Gooney Bird Greene announced.

"And these"—she gestured to the other children and they entered the room, marching, wearing their costumes of cardboard hats and headbands and belt buckles—"are Pilgrims and Native Americans.

"They are Squanto's friends," she added.

The Pilgrims and Native Americans stood in a semicircle behind Gooney Bird. They all adjusted their headgear and then stood with their hands at their sides, wiggling their eyebrows to hold up their hats and headbands, which were already slipping forward on their foreheads.

"Now, in honor of Thanksgiving, I am going to tell you a story," Gooney Bird said.

Mrs. Pidgeon played a "ta-DA" chord on the piano. The audience clapped and laughed. All of them knew already, because they had been told by their children, what a good storyteller Gooney Bird Greene was. Even Barbara Greene, Gooney Bird's mom, clapped and laughed.

From behind his headband, which had settled across his nose, Malcolm muttered, "I hope they don't clap too loud and wake up those triplets."

Gooney Bird took a few deep breaths, adjusted her posture, and began.

I am not the actual Squanto. The real Squanto was a Patuxet Indian who was born in a village near where the Pilgrims would land, but when he was born they hadn't landed yet.

He learned to speak English from some early settlers. He helped them in many ways. He was a very helpful guy.

When some of them went back to England, they invited him to go along. His mother didn't want him to.

I can understand that. My mom wouldn't want me to go off to another country. She would say I was too young. We would probably have a big argument about it.

"Oops," Gooney Bird said. "That was an authorial intrusion. I didn't mean to do that. It's boring."

But he went anyway. This was way back in the 1600s. Squanto is dead now. I am not the real Squanto. I am an imitation.

"Mr. Leroy?" Gooney Bird said. "Could you tell us the meaning of *imitation*, please?"

The principal looked up and cleared his throat. "Well, ah," he said with a nervous little laugh. "It means *fake*. You are a fake Squanto."

Gooney Bird looked behind her at the semicircle of Pilgrims and Native Americans. "Barry?" she said. Barry, pushing his headband up on his forehead, stepped forward.

"Imitation," Barry said in a loud voice. *"Something made to be as much as possible like something else."* He bowed and stepped back. Everyone, including Mr. Leroy, clapped.

"Thank you, Barry," Gooney Bird said. To the audience, she explained, "Mrs. Pidgeon has taught us all to use a dictionary. We have gotten very good at it, for second-graders, because we didn't underestimate ourselves.

"Underestimate? Beanie?" Gooney Bird said.

Beanie stepped forward. She stumbled a bit, because her hat was over her eyes. Then she righted herself, stood straight, and said, *"Underestimate. To judge things as less than their real value."* She curtsied, and whispered, "Like I underestimated the bigness of my hat."

The audience laughed and clapped. Gooney Bird continued the story.

After a while, Squanto got tired of being in

England. It was noisy and everybody went shopping all the time. He was homesick. So he cajoled a sea captain into taking him back to America.

"Felicia Ann," Gooney Bird announced. Felicia Ann, her Pilgrim bonnet completely covering her eyes and nose, stepped forward shyly.

"Cajole. To persuade someone to do something, by flattery or gentle argument," she said in her small voice.

The audience clapped. Gooney Bird continued.

He traveled around for a while, being helpful because he was a helpful guy. He was an interpreter between the Americans and the Indians—

"Malcolm?" Gooney Bird said. *"Interpreter?"*

Malcolm unbent his green feather, straightened his headband, and wiggled his fingers the way he always did when he was nervous. He hesitated a moment, thinking. Then he said, *"Interpreter. Someone who translates something from one language to another and helps people understand each other."*

The audience clapped.

"Shhh," Malcolm told them, with his fingers to his lips. "Don't clap too loud."

But suddenly—

The children smiled in anticipation at the *suddenly*.

—a bad ship captain tricked him into going onto his ship. It was a big scam. They made him a captive and took him to Spain. The captives all were sold as slaves. It made Squanto pretty mad.

But he was indefatigable.

Gooney Bird grinned. "Tyrone?" she said.

Tyrone, his headband completely covered in beads and with two feathers attached, strutted forward proudly. *"Indefatigable,"* he proclaimed. *"Never showing any sign of getting tired!"*

"Thank you, Tyrone," said Gooney Bird, after the applause. "I'm going to flash forward a bit now. That's a thing authors do."

After a long time Squanto finally made his way home. He had been away for years. And when he finally got home, he found that his village was gone. His people had all died. He was the last of his tribe.

It was very sad. But he became friends with the great chief Massasoit, and after a while he met the

Pilgrims, who had just arrived. So he had some new friends and they hung out together.

The Pilgrims' lives in America would have been a fiasco if good Indians like Squanto had not helped them.

"Chelsea? *Fiasco?*"

Chelsea waved to her mother in the front row. *"Fiasco. A total failure."*

Chelsea curtsied, and gave a thumbs-up sign.

Gooney Bird finished her story.

Squanto had gotten lots of new clothes in England, and he had learned to dance.
      The End.

Gooney Bird bowed, twirled in a circle, and did a small bit of hula.

"All of my story was absolutely true, except maybe the part about learning to dance, but I think he probably did," Gooney Bird said.

The audience rose to their feet, clapping and cheering. From the back of the room, when the applause quieted, the sound of babies crying came from the huge stroller. Malcolm pulled his headband down over his eyes and groaned.

"I have a couple more things to say," Gooney Bird

announced. "The first Thanksgiving is a really good story because it tells about people becoming friends and being helpful to each other, and being thankful.

"So some of the second-graders want to say what they are thankful for. Nicholas?"

Nicholas said loudly, "The Muriel. I got to do the forest part. And Mrs. Pidgeon. She stretches our skills."

Next Gooney Bird said, "Keiko?"

"My family," Keiko said. "And Mrs. Pidgeon. She makes me smile."

"Ben?"

Ben hopped up and down. "My fixed broken arm." He held it up. "And Mrs. Pidgeon. I like her songs. And she lets us change socks."

"One more," Gooney Bird said, "and then we can have our refreshments. Malcolm?"

Malcolm sighed. Slowly he walked forward. He looked toward the big stroller. "Okay, I guess I'm thankful for my triplets," he said after a moment. "Their names are Taylor, Schuyler, and Tierney, and two are boys and one's a girl but I don't know which is which.

"And I'm thankful for Mrs. Pidgeon because she is very calm, even when I'm not.

"And I'm thankful for the room mother because she brought cupcakes, and I'm hungry."

From the back of the room, a voice called out. "I didn't

bring them. I *provided* them. There is a difference!"

Then, very slowly, an elderly woman stood, lifting herself up by the arms of her wheelchair. Next to her, a nurse reached out to steady the chair.

"Here is what I'm thankful for," the old woman continued. "I'm thankful that Gooney Bird Greene called me on the telephone and asked me to be room mother. I haven't been room mother for thirty-five years. I was room mother when my daughter Patsy was in second grade. It was fun then, and it will be fun now.

"And mostly I am thankful that Patsy became a teacher. It makes me proud."

She lifted one hand and waved to Mrs. Pidgeon, seated at the piano. Mrs. Pidgeon dabbed her eyes with a hanky and then waved back. "Hi, Mom," she said with a smile.

"And don't forget, Gooney Bird Greene, " the room mother said, "you promised me a special song."

Gooney Bird looked at Mrs. Pidgeon.

"Class?" Mrs. Pidgeon said, and played the first chord.

"Roooommmm Motherrrr," the children sang.

THE END